Airdrie
Marigold Library System
NOV 1 9 2019

D0119215

Milton & Odie

and the Bigger-than-Bigmouth Bass

To all the optimists who give others hope

Copyright © 2019 by Mary Ann Fraser
All rights reserved, including the right of reproduction in whole or in part in any form.
Charlesbridge and colophon are registered trademarks of Charlesbridge Publishing, Inc.

At the time of publication, all URLs printed in this book were accurate and active.
Charlesbridge and the author are not responsible for the content or accessibility of
any website.

Published by Charlesbridge
85 Main Street, Watertown, MA 02472
(617) 926-0329 • www.charlesbridge.com

Library of Congress Cataloging-in-Publication Data
Names: Fraser, Mary Ann, author, illustrator.
Title: Milton & Odie and the bigger-than-bigmouth bass / Mary Ann Fraser.
Other titles: Milton and Odie and the bigger-than-bigmouth bass
Description: Watertown, MA: Charlesbridge, [2019] | Summary: Milton the pessimist
    and Odie the optimist are two otters living on opposite sides of a frozen lake, and
    neither one is having much luck at ice fishing—until they meet up and join forces.
Identifiers: LCCN 2018053879 (print) | LCCN 2018060228 (ebook) |
    ISBN 9781632898517 (ebook) | ISBN 9781632898524 (ebook pdf) |
    ISBN 9781623540982 (reinforced for library use)
Subjects: LCSH: Otters—Juvenile fiction. | Ice fishing—Juvenile fiction. | Cooperativeness—
    Juvenile fiction. | Sharing—Juvenile fiction. | CYAC: Otters—Fiction. | Ice fishing—
    Fiction. | Fishing—Fiction. | Cooperativeness—Fiction. | Sharing—Fiction.
Classification: LCC PZ7.F86455 (ebook) | LCC PZ7.F86455 Mi 2019 (print) | DDC 813.54
    [E]—dc23
LC record available at https://lccn.loc.gov/2018053879

Printed in China
(hc) 10 9 8 7 6 5 4 3 2 1

Illustrations done in gouache, crayon, and pencil on paper
Display type set in Imperfectly by Mats-Peter Forss
Text type set in Bembo by Adobe Systems Incorporated
Color separations by Colourscan Print Co Pte Ltd, Singapore
Printed by 1010 Printing International Limited in Huizhou, Guangdong, China
Production supervision by Brian G. Walker
Designed by Diane M. Earley

Milton & Odie

and the Bigger-than-Bigmouth Bass

BIG FISH LAKE

FISH AT YOUR OWN RISK

Mary Ann Fraser

Charlesbridge

Airdrie Public Library
111–304 Main Street S
Airdrie, Alberta T4B 3C3

Milton stumbles out of bed and swipes the frost from his window.

"*Bah!* What a miserable day for ice fishing!"

Odie leaps out of bed to check the weather.

"*Aah!* What a beautiful day to test my luck on the lake!"

Milton drills a hole, hooks a worm,
and dunks his tangled line.

Kerplunk!
In the lonely stillness he waits.
And nothing.
Not a nibble.
Not a bobble.
Not a bite.

Odie saws a hole, hooks a worm,
and lets his sleek line sink.

Kerplink!

In the splendid stillness he waits.

And nothing.

Not a nibble.

Not a bobble.

Not a bite.

"Bet this lake has nothing worth catching,"
Milton mumbles.

He hauls up his line.

"No wonder there's no nibble. This worm has no wiggle. I'll try bait with more jiggle."

Milton plucks a red thread from his sock. "*Pew!* This stinky string will have to do."

Kerplunk.

"Bet this lake is brimming with big catches,"
Odie sings.

He reels in his line.

"No wonder there's no nibble. This weary worm needs a rest. I'll try bait with more zest."

He pulls a stick of gooseberry gum from his pocket. "Yum! *Gum* and get it, fishies!"

Kerplink!

Milton's bobber bobs. His pole bends.
He gives a yank and pulls an old sole
from the hole.

"Just my luck. A yucky, mucky boot."

Odie's bobber bobs. His pole bends.

He gives a heave and lands a very wet net.

"What great luck! A super fish scooper."

Milton feels even less hopeful. Still, he drops in his line again.

Kerplunk.

Odie knows something even
better waits below. He drops in
his line again, of course.

Kerplink!

Milton checks his watch.

His bobber bobs. His pole bends.

"*Ugh!* I've snagged the bottom."

He gives a yank and reels back the slack.

Odie hums a merry tune.

His bobber bobs. His pole bends.

"*Woohoo!* I've hooked a big one!"

He gives a heave but can't hang on . . .

Milton pulls Odie's pole up through the hole!

"What good are two poles when there are no fish?" Milton kicks his bucket and heads for home.

"Time to fetch another pole." Odie scoops
up his bucket and springs for home.

By chance, Milton and
Odie meet.

"Hey, you found my pole!"
Odie exclaims.

"Hey, your gum stuck to my thread,"
Milton grumbles.

"Care to join me?" asks Odie. "I'm fishing for a bigmouth bass."

"How do you know there's one down there?" asks Milton.

"How do you know there *isn't?*" asks Odie.

Milton had never asked himself that before.

For just a second, Milton imagines what might be below the ice.

He drills a new hole, hooks a worm, and dunks his tangled line.

Kerplunk!

Odie saws a new hole, hooks a worm,
and lets his sleek line sink.

Kerplink!

In the stillness they wait.

"I have a not-so-little nibble!" Milton shouts.

"I have a bigger-than-big bobble!" Odie hollers.

Milton gives a yank.

Odie gives a heave.

They reel back their slack and . . .

together they net a *bigger*-than-bigmouth bass!

"Why are you still fishing?" Odie asks. "We've already caught a *bigger*-than-bigmouth bass."

"How do we know there isn't another one down there?" Milton asks.

"That's the spirit!" cheers Odie.

And so, together . . .

. . . they imagine the possibilities.